MY BIG DADDY GOT ME

DOMINIC

JUST BAE

ISBN: 978-1-925988-52-9

CONTENTS

CHAPTER 1

Dominic came downstairs, looking for his wife, Bernadette and found her standing out on the balcony of their hotel room. Picking up his leather jacket over the railing, he went to the door and stepped outside.

"It's cold out here, honey," he said draping his jacket over his wife's shoulders, then wrapping his arms around her.

"I know honey," Bernadette said,

leaning back against Dominic. "But it is so lovely out here. The view is amazing."

"Yes, it is," Dominic said, kissing Bernadette as they watched as the sunset painted the snow-capped peaks. "We have a few hours before Christmas. What should we do?"

"I'd love to go for a walk with my prince charming," Bernadette said, pointing down below to the back of the hotel where there was an ice-skating rink with a few couples hanging out.

"Your wish is my command, love," Dominic said, kissing Bernadette's cheek.

"Let's get dressed."

"Ok, sweetheart."

AFTER A HALF-HOUR, the couple and their escort, Bill left the hotel onto the snow and followed the winding path finally ending up at the rink. They watched the skaters for a few minutes and then Dominic said, "Would a noblewoman of your grace like to go ice skating?"

"I'd love to with you, my prince."

Dominic lifted Bernadette's mitten to his lips. "I'll go and get the skates," he said, brushing kissing her hand.

"Hey Bill, do you skate?" Bernadette said to her long-time personal bodyguard. Bernadette was a celebrity fashion designer.

"I do. For four years on my high school's hockey team."

"Three pairs then. What sizes?" Dominic said.

"I already know. Ladies-Nine and for you, Bill?"

"A ten, Dominic. Thanks."

"No problem, bud.

Dominic headed to the rental booth and minutes later, he and Bernadette were gliding hand in hand, melding in with the other skaters. Bill followed them, watchful of any suspicious activity.

Dominic spun his wife around, skating backward as he pulled her along. "Have you seen the women trying to get Bill to skate with them?"

"I have, poor Bill."

"I see they've stopped trying now. They must think he's gay," Dominic said and Bernadette giggled.

"Maybe, it's always the good-looking ones getting picked on."

* * *

THEY SKATED for about an hour and then left. They returned down the winding path until coming upon a lighted area where some clearing had been set up with wooden chairs and barrels. A fire was burning and people were sitting around it.

"Oh, Dominic, look it's a live nativity," Bernadette said, taking in the outdoor scene of a manger with live sheep and goats. "Can we stay for a bit?"

"Of course we can, my love." Dominic leaned down to kiss his wife's nose. There was a notice that the next show was in about ten minutes. The trio moved to find seats as close to the front as possible.

The lights lining the seating area went out, leaving only one bright one directly above the manger. Some music came on and the performance began.

Dominic missed most of what was going on; he was too busy watching Bernadette. Her face was lit in childish wonder as a retelling of the special birth was played out.

When the performance came to an

end and the light above the set went out, a hush fell over the crowd – the moment was a special one.

* * *

"Oh, that was beautiful," Bernadette kept saying as they made their way back to the hotel, her head leaning on Dominic's shoulder.

"Yes, it was," Dominic said.

"I'll tell our niece, Louisa. I know she would love it. It would be lovely to have something like that in our back yard, don't you think?"

"It would," Dominic said just as they reached the back of the hotel. "Before we go inside there is something I have to do. I promised Louisa. It was a part of this Christmas getaway she planned for us," Dominic said grinning.

"And what's that?" Bernadette said, turning.

"This." Dominic bent down and took some snow. Seeing what Dominic was about to do, Bernadette held up her hands.

"Don't you dare, Mr. Collins."

Dominic formed a snowball and slowly went to Bernadette. "Why not honey?" he said, tossing the snowball back and forth in his hands.

"Because… Dominic…," Bernadette said backing away.

"Well, you have to give me a reason," he said, lobbing the ball from hand to hand.

"Because I'll kill you."

Dominic stayed silent for a moment and then said, "I'll sacrifice my life over it." He threw the snowball, deliberately missing Bernadette.

"Bill? Help!" Bernadette said.

"Sorry, Ma'am. You're on your own. I'm staying out of this one."

"Coward," she said quickly diving to make a snowball.

Snowballs were sailing and the couple played until Bernadette said enough.

* * *

THE TELEPHONE WOKE DOMINIC. He groaned as he rolled over Bernadette, to answer it.

"Hello."

"Merry Christmas, Uncle Dominic." It was Louisa. Dominic winced a little at the volume in her voice and said, "Merry Christmas, sweetheart." He got out of bed, the long cord on the phone followed him to the window. He began speaking softly not to wake Bernadette.

"Yes—yes—well. She's still sleeping… I'll have her call you when she gets up."

"I am up, Bill," Bernadette said. When Dominic turned around, she said, "Looks like I'm not the only one."

"Who's that?"

"Hey, sexy. Behave yourself," Dominic whispered as he brought the phone over. "Your niece might hear something." As Bernadette spoke to Louisa, Dominic put on some tight candy-cane boxers Bernadette got him the night before.

Bernadette put her hands over her mouth watching Dominic's crotch erect. She stuck out her tongue as Dominic walked to the bathroom. When he came out, Bernadette was still on the phone. Dominic then went downstairs to make some coffee.

DOMINIC WAS ON THE SOFA, drinking and

munching on fruitcake when Bernadette came down.

"I'm so sorry, darling," she said as she reached the bottom of the stairs. "You know Louisa. Our niece is a talker."

"I do," Dominic said. "I made you some tea."

"What time is it?"

"About six."

"Hmm, I knew there was a reason why I married you." Bernadette kissed Dominic and laid beside him.

"Santa's in town—" Dominic gestured downward.

"I see," she said picking up her teacup.

* * *

AFTER THEY ATE BREAKFAST, Dominic put on a Santa hat. Bernadette giggled while passing out the gifts from under the tree. She waited to open hers until they were all piled on the coffee table; hers in front of her and Dominic's in front of him.

"Wishful thinking, Mr. Collins?" she said laughing as she opened the first gift – pulling out green silky cami, matching bra and g-string.

"Can't blame a man for trying," Dominic said chuckling as he opened his first gift; a watch.

"There's something written in the back," Bernadette said as she set the box of lingerie aside and picked up the next present from him. Dominic pulled the watch out and turned it over. "For all time," he read, "All my love, Bernadette."

"Wow, this is perfect, sweetheart," Dominic said drawing Bernadette's mouth to his to kiss. "Thank you, my love."

"You're welcome," she said unwrapping another gift in her lap. She pulled the top off the square-shaped jeweler's box and gasped, "Oh, Dominic."

"I wanted you to have something to remember our time here."

"Oh, baby. It's gorgeous." Bernadette exhaled pulling the necklace out; at its end was a diamond-studded snowflake. She bent over and Dominic slipped it around her neck then gently kissed her forehead.

"I knew it was for you the moment I saw it."

Bernadette squeezed his hand as she turned to open several more. The last gift had a card attached to it reading: "You hold the key to my heart." She opened it and inside was another necklace but the pendant on this one was a key – made from white gold covered in sapphires and diamonds.

"Dominic, oh my God!"
"You like it, huh?"

"Hell yeah!" Bernadette kissed Dominic nonstop. "Thank you."

"You are welcome, my love."

* * *

ONE LAST GIFT, which was the largest, was hanging off the table for Dominic. He opened the card seeing his wife's hand in salutation.

"The music of my life began with you," It read. Dominic looked surprised as he began removing the wrapping paper.

"All you talked about was getting another guitar," Bernadette said as Dominic pulled the guitar out of the box. "I found an artisan in town—he makes them by hand in his shop. I knew when I saw them, it would be the perfect gift."

Dominic put the guitar against the table and reached out, pulling Bernadette until she was in his arms. "Thank you, my love," he said before kissing her.

Bernadette tucked her head up licking his ear feeling the warmness of her husband's torso against her.

"Well, since you're already dressed for a performance, won't you do one for me?"

"My pleasure."

Dominic played some of Bruce Springsteen's hits next to the fireplace. Bernadette was curled up in one of the armchairs while Dominic sat in another playing for his wife long into the morning.

It was noon when they headed upstairs to shower. Friends and family texted Bernadette during Dominic's mini-guitar performance saying they would like to get together for Christmas dinner.

CHAPTER 2

"It's been a very long time since I've been pampered," Bernadette said to Amy as they left the spa, heading down towards the elevator.

"You should do this more often, girl. You deserve it."

"Maybe, I should. I have time now that Louisa's running my day-to-day stuff at Bene in town." Bernadette chuckles. "Life isn't quite as busy as it was when I was running things all by myself. I couldn't even think about having an hour to get my nails done even on a day off."

"I hear you, girl."

They were near the elevators when they passed the 'ladies room' sign.

"Hey, I'm supposed to meet Dominic at the fireplace," Bernadette said. "I don't want to head all the way upstairs to use the bathroom," she turned to her body-guard standing behind them. "Mark, I'll be going inside."

"Yes, ma'am."

"I'm going back up and rest a bit before we have dinner," Amy said yawning.

"Of course, dear," Bernadette said. "You go on ahead I'll see you later."

"Alright." Amy headed to the eleva-tors. Once she got on, Bernadette turned to Mark.

"Shall we," she said. Mark nodded and led the way. "Wait, while I check things out."

"Okie-dokie."

"Hello! Anyone inside?" Mark stepped in while Bernadette checked her phone.

"It's all clear, Ma'am. I'll be here"

"Thank you, Mark."

* * *

"YOU KNOW that I let you win, right?" Mark's nephew, Anthony said as he and Dominic left the pool hall.

"Keep telling yourself that," Dominic said tapping the young man on the shoulder. "I beat you fair and square. Face it, boy…you suck."

"Come on, uncle. You don't have to rub it in." Anthony said. "I'll bet my aunt can beat you."

"Oh, she beats me in a lot of things but no pool." Dominic said, amused by the look on Anthony's face. He was just about to say something when out of the corner of his eye he saw Mark standing in front of ladies' room.

"Hey, Dominic," Mark said smiling.

"Hey, bud. Are the ladies inside?"

"Only Bernadette, sir. Amy went back up to the suite."

Dominic nodded and Mark stepped aside allowing Dominic to enter. As the door closed, he heard the lock click and Anthony put his hand over his mouth. "I'd wait in the lobby with little Anthony if I were you. You wouldn't want to hear anything that would compromise us."

"Yes, sir." Mark blushed and went with Anthony to the lobby.

* * *

DOMINIC LEANED against the door inside and waited.

"Think being with me and leaving

Uncle Don and Aunt Bernie alone is okay?" Anthony said.

"Yeah, son. Why would you say that?" Mark looked for a place to make sure they could be close but not too far.

"I guess you would say that." Anthony laughed. "Let's just say that when I get my uncle's age, I hope I'll have half the energy he does."

"You're making it seem like you and I are dead."

"Pretty much," Anthony said. "I'll leave the lovebirds for you to watch. I'm going upstairs. See you tonight, Mark."

"Ok, bud."

* * *

BERNADETTE CAME out and was at the sink. Dominic smiled as he made sure the door was locked.

"Hello, stranger," she said, seeing her hubby in the mirror.

"Hello," Dominic said as he came closer. "How was your spa day?"

"Beautiful, thanks for asking."

Dominic came behind her and put his hands on her shoulder. He then kissed her shoulder.

"My lady, you smell good," Dominic growled as he nuzzled the curve of Bernadette's neck and shoulder.

"It's the cherry almond oil the masseuse put on me." Bernadette tilted her head to the side. "Maybe I should go more often."

"Definitely," Dominic growled as he grasped her chin and tilted her head back. His mouth captured hers.

Their tongues tangled battling for dominance – lunging and parrying, thrusting and retreating in an erotic imitation of the more intimate act they were craving.

As the kissing went on, Dominic's hand slid from Bernadette's chin down through the open neck of her blouse to grab her breast. Bernadette arched, pressing herself deeper into his grasp.

When she was about to turn around, Dominic pulled his lips from hers.

"Don't move," he panted against her cheek. Bernadette only nodded and Dominic's tongue darted swiftly back into her mouth.

"My love," he breathed pointing to the mirror and Bernadette lifted her gaze to meet his in the mirror watching his hands slowly unbuttoning her blouse. Dominic then pulled the fabric out of the waistband of her pants and parted the silky fabric. Pushing it back off Bernadette's shoulders, his hands skimmed up her torso to the front of her green lacy bra; his Christmas gift. Dominic unfastened the clasp and peeled the cups off. "My God!" he said as her breasts bounced satisfying his hungry gaze.

Bernadette moaned feeling Dominic playing with her breasts and teasing her nipples. "Dominic…" she breathed as her hands slid to grasp his ass pulling him in.

Dominic's cock poked her backside. "This makes you wet?" he said biting Bernadette's earlobe.

She replied by taking his hand, sliding it down to the button closure of her pants. Dominic popped the button, slid down the zipper and growled something when he saw the green g-string in the mirror. Grasping the edges, he eased them down her hips and gave a push until they slid down to her feet. Bernadette kicked them aside, craving his touch where she burned for the most and took his hand to guide it.

Bernadette gasped and shivered as Dominic's fingers glided over her mound finding the slickness of her desire. "My God! You're so wet—" His fingers then parted her. Her hips bucked the instant he touched her clit, rubbing it with his thumb. Dominic slid two fingers deep inside and massaged gently. Bernadette's moans grew as he stroked. The sweet torture went on until she could take it anymore.

"Dominic… god, Dominic please," Bernadette gasped as she dropped her hand to grab his wrist while he was still fingering. "I need your cock now, please big daddy…Oh my God—"

He obeyed kissing her as he fumbled for his belt, then the button and finally the zipper.

"Hurry—daddy   before   I—"

Bernadette moaned, pulling her mouth from his as she reached to help him as he shoved his jeans and boxers down. "Lean forward." Bernadette, of course, complied. Widening and bracing her hands on the countertop, he put the head of his cock along her lips, coating himself with her pussy then positioned himself. With one thrust, Big Daddy entered.

"Fuck—Yes. Daddy…" Bernadette shouted.

Dominic began thrusting, bending forward stretching his body until he laid against her back, pressing his mouth to the back of her neck; his hot breath against her skin. Bernadette turned, seeking his and he captured her kiss; his tongue moved in and out in rhythm to the slow pumping. One hand rested firmly against her chest, keeping her pressed to him and as he felt his ejaculation building along with Bernadette's. He took his free hand, stroking her clit as he rode.

"Oh god, Big D…Dominic… like that…yes… yes." Bernadette moaned as she rocked to his rhythm.

Dominic knew she was close to coming. He took her earlobe between his teeth, nibbled and growled. "Come for big daddy, come for big D—"

"D…Dominic…"

He felt her walls contracting around him. "Come, baby" he growled as he squeezed her clit. That was enough to send Bernadette over the edge. She screamed his name as she came, her walls clutching and pulling at him, relentlessly massaging his hardness as he picked up the pace of his stabbing, plunging harder and faster as he strove for his own.

"Ah.. oh god…my love…" Dominic groaned his orgasm was just out of reach. Bernadette pushed herself up so she could slide her hand down and grasped his nuts, giving it a squeeze. "Come for me now," she said gently rolling his balls in her hand.

"Ah, Bernadette…" Dominic growled as he came, spilling into her as his body spasmed. Dominic clung on, kissing as the waves of pleasure slowly ebbed.

"Oh god," he lifted Bernadette from her waist.

"You can say that again." Bernadette kissed Dominic's forehead. "I don't think we've ever made love in front of the mirror in a public bathroom before."

"There's a first time for everything."

"We should head up to the room before dinner," she said between kisses.

"I think you're right."

Once dressed, Dominic slipped his arm around Bernadette and led her to the door.

He turned the lock, opening the door

and Dominic chuckled when he saw Mark waiting in the lobby, the poor guy was looking a little green around the gills.

"You okay there, Mark?" Bernadette said.

Dominic grinned as he took Bernadette's hand and tucked it inside his arm.

"Yes, sir," Mark said clearing his throat. He blushed as the couple approached.

"Great. Let's get ready for the evening," Dominic said and Mark led them toward the elevators.

When the couples finished dinner and exchanged their goodbyes, Bernadette gasped when she saw what was parked in front of their vehicle.

"Dominic," she said. "What's in the world!"

"I thought my lovely wife would like a sleigh ride up the mountain to the Springs." A large sleigh pulled by a team of Clydesdales.

Dominic led Bernadette over to the sleigh.

"Good evening, sir, ma'am," The driver said, turning around in the rider's seat, holding red leather reins.

"Evening." Dominic smiled as he helped Bernadette up.

"You'll find a thermos of hot chocolate and a couple of mugs in the box underneath the seats. The wife makes the best hot chocolate in the town. I'm Jacob, by the way… but you can just call me Jay," the man said as he turned back to face the horses.

"Thank you. We're Dominic and Bernadette."

Dominic and Bernadette settled into their places taking a woolen blanket beside them and spreading it over their laps; tucking the ends in to keep out the chill.

"All settled back there?"

"Yes, thank you," Dominic said as he put his arm around Bernadette.

"Alright then," Jacob said flicking the reins of the horses. The bells on their harnesses jingled in the night air.

Bernadette laid on Dominic's shoulder and he kissed her forehead. "Happy, my love?"

"Blissfully," she said as she tucked her head inside.

"Good." Dominic kissed Bernadette underneath the blanket while holding her hand and enjoying the beauty of the ride up the mountain. Occasionally, the calm was interrupted by their driver giving them a bit of history and trivia about the area they were going through.

Thirty minutes later, the sleigh pulled up to the entrance of the outdoor pool and two-story bathhouse.

"Here you are. I hope you enjoyed the ride," Jacob said.

"It was lovely, thank you, Jacob," Bernadette said.

Dominic got out first and helped his wife down. "Do you wish me to stay for the return?" Jacob said.

"No, thank you. We'll be okay," Dominic said giving Jacob a tip. "Thanks again for the ride and Happy Holidays."

"You do the same, sir."

THE BODYGUARDS FOLLOWED the couple as they went up the steps to the bathhouse. As they approached, the door opened. Once inside, a receptionist greeted them.

"Welcome to the Cascade Upper Hot Springs. I'm the director of the Springs. As per the request of your security team, the Springs has been closed to everyone. I'll be in my office over there if you need anything. Please enjoy."

"Thank you." Bernadette smiled.

Their head guard for the evening, Mark turned to Dominic. "I'll keep two guards here at the door. The rest of us will patrol the building. According to the blueprint, there are no other entrances to the Springs except by climbing up the fence which has cameras everywhere," he said. "But if you want I can have my men outside to keep watch."

"No, I think what you have in place will be just fine," Dominic said.

"Great." Mark smiled watching as Dominic took Bernadette's arm and walked with her toward the changing area. They left each other; Dominic to the men's change room and Bernadette to the ladies.

The couple dressed up in robes given to them by the resort's staff along with flip-flops. When they got to the door of the pool, Bernadette began shivering.

Dominic hugged her as they made their way to the pool. Bernadette dipped her foot in.

"Ooh…"

"Too hot?"

"Oh no," Bernadette said as she untied her robe, dropping on the tile. As the cold air hit her skin she shivered and then quickly got in the water, sinking below until only her head was above water. "Oh it's lovely, baby," she sighed as the heat from the water pierced her body. Bernadette swam until she reached the center. When she came up, she brushed her hair back and turned to Dominic who still stood at the ledge. "Care to join me, Big Daddy?"

"Is that a name you just said one day you'll pick out for me, Miss?"

"Maybe," Bernadette said winking. "Why don't you come in here and find out."

"Well, I'm not one to pass up a challenge, especially one that involves steam and water." Dominic grinned taking off his robe. He dived in, swimming over to Bernadette. Once he reached, he pulled her in closer. "Now, what were you saying?"

Bernadette leaned and pressed her lips to his. It was a brief and light kiss and then she slipped from his arms. "Now you have to catch me," she said diving underneath and swimming away. Dominic laughed and swam after her.

They played a game of chase and keep away for a few minutes until Bernadette let Dominic catch her. He grabbed her ankle and pulled her back. She came up and Dominic pulled her right into his arms. "See, Big Daddy knows how to catch his fish."

"Mmm, I see you do," Bernadette said as she put her arms around him. "Now that you've caught me, what are you going to do?"

"Oh! I'm sure I'll think of something," he said running his fingers dancing up and down the curve of her back.

"Oooh! I'm sure you will," she said shivering to his touch.

"Wrap your legs around me," Dominic said helping her. While hugging, he carried Bernadette over to the end of the pool to the area of the steps. He set her down until she was seated halfway out of the water. When Dominic would have kneeled, Bernadette said, "Lay back. I have a better idea."

Bernadette moved close to the hot length of Dominic's cock while Dominic's hands were on her back holding her in position. The water's steam made it so as if she was almost floating over him. Dominic kissed first and their tongues began tangling, parrying and thrusting.

Dominic's lips then trailed down a hot path to Bernadette's breast. Taking in the nipple, Big Daddy suckled greedily. Bernadette titled her head back and moaned. After a long sequence, Bernadette dropped her head forward, resting it against his as her hands slid from his backside to the front and down to his cock.

Dominic sang out with a low moan as her hand jerked him, bringing him close to the edge of an orgasm.

Pulling his lips off her breast he moaned, "Bernadette, fuck—" He squirmed as he was about to cum. "Stop—"

Right before he did, Bernadette released it and then braced her hands on his shoulders arching herself up. Dominic's held her as she lowered herself onto his cock until it was sheathed deep inside.

"Wow, Big Daddy—" she purred and began moving slowly, setting the pace. Dominic mimicked, and their bodies were in sync, as their arousal built.

"I love you," she said panting.

"I love you more," he said, kissing her. "You are my life. Fuck—" he couldn't finish saying his words feeling the perfect bending of Bernadette's back and the tensing of her vagina indicating she was close to coming.

"Oh God! Oh God! Fuck me, Dominic. Fuck me. I'm—" Bernadette screamed moving frantically as she strove for her climax.

Dominic thought that if he died right then and there, he would be a very happy man. There was no sight bt to him of more pleasure than that of his wife coming while being in his arms. She yelled his name as her climax hit, her body bucking and shuddering and that was enough to make him come almost at the same time.

They held each other for several minutes before Bernadette broke the silence between them.

"I could stay here like this forever but I suppose we'd best get out before Anthony and the others rush in here believing we've been attacked."

"No," he joked. "They'll just think we've finally died from all the sex we've been having on this trip."

"Dominic, you're so bad. What would I do without you?" Bernadette said hitting his shoulder. "You're so naughty."

"I am? "He said. "But that's why you love me isn't it?"

"Love you? Where did you get that from?" Bernadette said leaning back. "What makes you think I love you?" She giggled catching the playful look in Dominic's eyes just before he lifted her off him.

"Dominic, what are you doing?"

"This." He carried her and then tossed her into the water.

"Oh, you are a dead man, Dominic Collins," she said, wagging her finger.

"I'm so scared," Dominic said winking. When he lunged forward, Bernadette swam away. Big Daddy began the chase once again.

* * *

GERARD, Amy's husband looked at his watch again, sighing then turned to Amy. "Maybe you should go and get the two lovebirds."

"Me? Why me?"

"Because Dominic won't kill you for interrupting," he said.

"No way—I'm not going?" Amy said.

"Come on, baby—please honey sugar pie? Besides Dominic will have my head if I saw him and Bernadette fucking. I have business dealings with him, you know."

"And what about me? I'm his wife's bestie." Gerard stares at his wife. "No… no… no way…I'm not going. There's no way in hell and back that you can make me."

Gerald stared again resembling a cute puppy.

"Oh, all right. Stop looking at me like that. You owe me, Mr. G. Big time. I want you to—"

"Ok—I'll give you the G treatment tonight. Just go. I'll meet you in the lobby."

Amy put on her coat and headed to the Springs.

* * *

JUST AS AMY ARRIVED, the doors to the change rooms opened and the couple stepped out.

"Um—Hi," Amy smiled. "Gerard was beginning to worry."

"Really?" Bernadette smiled. "We weren't in there that long, were we?"

"Nearly two hours," Amy said.

"Wow, it really didn't seem that long," Dominic said as they walked back towards the main entrance meeting Gerard. "I hear you were worried about us, bud." Dominic chuckled.

"Huh, me?"

"You didn't send Amy to go in there after us, did you?" Bernadette said nearly laughing at the reaction Amy gave Gerard.

"Let's head back to the hotel," Dominic said as he held out his arm to Bernadette.

"Yes, my love," she said taking his

arm. As they went towards the exit, Bernadette turned around seeing Amy and Anthony still standing. "Are you two coming or not?"

Amy looked at Gerard and saw in his eyes what exactly what he was going to say.

"Don't you even!"

"Who me?"

Amy said something under her breath and the couple followed along.

* * *

"I can't believe we are almost at the end of our vacation already," Bernadette said as she finished getting ready for the New Year's Eve Ball.

"I know right," Dominic said going into the bedroom to get his shoes.

Meanwhile, Bernadette was looking in the mirror. She usually had a stylist do her hair but she'd given the girls time off for the holidays.

She finished putting on her makeup and then opened her jewelry box taking out the necklace Dominic had bought her for Christmas. After putting it on, she put the box back into the hotel room's safe.

The doorbell rang.

"That's Amy and Gerald," Dominic said as he came up beside her, resting his hands on her. "Are you ready?"

"As I'll ever be," Bernadette turned around kissing him. Taking her hand, Dominic led her to the front door.

THE COUPLES STOPPED outside the ballroom while Mark ordered his security team to enter first and position themselves. Gerard and Amy preceded them, the two bodyguards on watch, Bill and Carlos, and then followed by Dominic and Bernadette.

"Where's Anthony, Amy?" Bernadette said.

"You know he's upstairs playing online with his friends."

"Oh, okay."

Just as they stepped through the doorway into the ballroom the announcer said, "We'd like to welcome our special guests, Bernadette Collins of Bene and husband Dominic."

The couple stood for a moment in the doorway, accepting the applause that followed the announcement, and then they went into the ballroom.

Bernadette had accepted a flute of champagne when she heard her name being called. Bill and Carlos stepped up to flank her, but when she saw who was running through the crowd, she smiled and motioned them back.

"Bernadette, Bernadette," Kathryn said running forward.

"Well—hello, Kathryn." Bernadette said as she knelt to face the little girl, playing with her curls.

"Excuse me for a moment, my love… I see another young lady who has caught my eye," Dominic said. Bernadette frowned but then smiled when she saw him stop in front of Kathryn and bow.

"May I have the pleasure of this dance, Miss Kathryn," Dominic said. Kathryn giggled and looked back at her mother. Vanessa nodded and smiled with Dominic as he took her daughter's hand and led her out onto the dance floor.

As Dominic began dancing with Kathryn, Vanessa went over to where Bernadette and Amy were.

Bernadette grinned when she saw Kathryn looking up at Dominic.

"Looks like my hubby has stolen another girl's heart," Amy said.

"My husband has that effect on women," Bernadette said watching the two.

"He's so good with her," Vanessa said.

"Yes, he would have made a wonderful father," Bernadette said.

"And he is a fabulous dancer," Vanessa said seeming not to have heard Bernadette's comment.

"You have no idea," Amy said. "I walked in on the two of them one day dancing… Ooh boy!"

"Really?" Vanessa said.

"Yeah," Amy said. "Just wait until they get into it. They're just warming up."

After a few minutes, Kathryn ran back to her mother. "Mommy, Mommy —Mr. Dominic danced with me."

"I saw that sweetie," Vanessa said as she picked her daughter up and hugged her. Looking over her daughter's head, Vanessa said, "Thank you." Dominic gave her a thumbs-up. "How about we go and get something to eat?" Vanessa said to her daughter. "Ok, Mommy."

"Please excuse us."

Once Vanessa and Kathryn had left, Bernadette said to Dominic, "I see you've stolen another young lady's heart. I knew you were trouble when I first met you."

Dominic laughed, wrapping around Bernadette's waist. "There's only one girl's heart that matters."

"Oh you are such a sweet talker, mister," she said.

"Does this mean I'll get lucky tonight?" he said, his breath tickling Bernadette's ear.

"Oh, it's a pretty safe bet you will, Big

Daddy." Bernadette purred looking at him before turning her head.

Bernadette turned back to Amy who was beside her and began sipping from her wine glass. Looking back over her shoulder she spotted Mark standing with Bill against the wall. Turning back to Dominic, she leaned in and whispered something. Dominic leaned in glancing at Amy and then over his shoulder at Mark. He then said, "I'll take care of it."

"Good, my boy."

Dominic squeezed Bernadette's hand and stepped back, going over to stand on the other side of Mark.

He leaned in close and said, "So, are you just going to stand here all night looking at that woman or are you going to ask her to dance?"

"Dominic… I'm working, remember," Mark said.

"Yes, you are and work didn't stop me from dancing for the first time with Bernadette at the company's Christmas party when I was still an employee of Bene."

"And the difference was that you were dancing with the woman you had known for a decade. I wouldn't be."

"Mark—buddy," Dominic said facing him. "It's okay if you want to dance. We have enough detail tonight – go on. It's New Year's Eve and it's okay to have a little fun."

"I—I don't know."

"Mark, I guarantee nothing will happen – relax, buddy. Bill and the others are on guard. Go on—"

Mark appeared to be ready to protest but then said. "Thanks, boss."

"Anytime."

Mark went over to the attractive brunette while Bill leaned over and said,

"Geez, I thought he'd never find the nerve to ask that woman to dance."

"Me, either." Dominic chuckled then went back to Bernadette.

"Dance with me, my lady?" he said in her ear.

"Always," she smiled, holding out her hand out.

CHAPTER 4

As the music played, Dominic pulled Bernadette in closer and she snuggled. She closed her eyes, letting her other senses take over as Dominic led her through the steps. The pressure of his hand on her back felt good. His warmth sept through her body and chased along with her, making her insides tingle. She breathed in his scent of musk and spicy aftershave leaving her giddy.

"Hmm, Mr. Big Daddy's glad to see me. I feel," Bernadette said in his ear.

"You already know," Dominic said moving his lips up to her ear. "I want to fuck my beautiful wife."

"Mmm, what a coincidence because I want to fuck you too, husband," Bernadette said blowing hot air in his ear.

"What do you say we ditch this party and go fuck somewhere?"

"Mmm, that's the best thing you've said all day."

"You're going to have to walk in front of me though."

"And why's that?" Bernadette said giggling, knowing exactly what he meant.

"Hmm, because—" Dominic said. "This hard-on will get us in trouble. Do you want that?"

"Hmm, maybe I do." Bernadette's eyes dropped for a moment. When she lifted them, she was amazed licking her lips. "Oh, you're mine, buddy."

"If we don't go now while this room is full of people… I'm going to have to fuck you right here," he said.

"Oh my, you are a brave man," Bernadette said moving away from the heat. Dominic followed behind her and she faked a smile moving through the crowd.

One of the personal detail, Bill followed them closely to where Gerard and Amy were dancing.

"Having fun you two?" Bernadette said smiling.

"Of course."

"Good. Hubby and I are going to call it a night."

"It's almost midnight…you'll miss the countdown," Amy said. "And the fireworks."

"That's okay, dear. We'll watch them

from the balcony." Bernadette said, "Stay and enjoy the party."

When Bernadette and Dominic walked off, Gerard said, "Those two lovebirds can't stop fucking."

Bernadette chuckled. "I wish you did it to me at least half the time, they do."

* * *

AFTER SAYING THEIR GOODNIGHTS, the couple headed up to the room. At the door, Bernadette turned back to Bill. "Why don't you head back down to the party and find yourself a nice young lady to dance with."

"I'll try, ma'am." Bill smiled. "If you insist, but I don't think I'd have much luck."

"Oh, and why is that?" Bernadette said, raising her eyebrows, knowing there are women dying to be with anyone who works for her.

"Well, the girl I want is already taken," he said winking and going back down the hall.

"Good night, Bill. Happy New Year."

"Happy New Year, ma'am."

Bernadette closes the door.

"Oh, that Bill is going to give you a run for your money, my love," Bernadette said as she turned back to Dominic.

"Am I in danger of losing my spot in your infatuations, my love?" Dominic said as he took off his jacket.

"Never! You'll always be my number one no matter who sweet-talks me." Bernadette kissed Dominic as she breezed past him.

Just as Bernadette stepped into the parlor, they heard the fireworks from the lawn of the hotel. Bernadette stepped out onto the balcony, shivering, as the star-burst of colors peppered the night.

Dominic put his jacket over her shoulders and held her waist pulling her back.

They watched the fireworks until the last one. "Happy New Year, honey."

"Happy New Year, my darling," Bernadette said. Dominic bent over to kiss her.

"Shall we take this inside?"

"Yes, Big Daddy."

* * *

BERNADETTE SLOWLY AWOKE, and even without looking at the clock she knew it was still early. Dominic's arms were around her waist and he pulls her back against him.

"Again?" she said as she felt the heat of his cock pressing against her butt.

"Again and again, and again until morning and we're both too tired to move," Dominic said with his hand sliding sensuously up along her thigh.

"Mmm, but it's already morning," Bernadette said as she rolled over, turning until she was facing him. She put her leg over his, hooking her foot behind his butt to pull him closer. "You're a mess," she said after she kissed him.

"Only when it comes to you," Dominic said before running his fingers through her hair and kissing back. Their tongues began a sensual dance, twining together, lunging and retreating.

Dominic caressed each curve and hollow of Bernadette's body and began going lower.

Bernadette moaned when Dominic's finger went inside her. She was wet moaning deeper as his finger slid in and out then moving back up to her clit. Dominic kept stroking, slow and steady.

Bernadette leaned back allowing her hips to move in sync with his thrusting. She then joined Dominic, closing tightly around his hand with hers, as she began rubbing her clit. She moved in slow circles gradually picking up speed while Dominic kept fingering. "Big Daddy—"

Dominic felt Bernadette was about to come. He got on top of her and began stabbing. Bernadette gasped as he slid in and she wrapped her legs around him, locking her ankles together, and moving with him. "Fuck me—Daddy. Ooo, ooo—Yes, yes. Right there, right there—"

Their mouths fused; tongues tangling hungrily, swallowing moans and gasps of pleasure.

With each thrust, Bernadette was nearing a major climax.

Knowing her body as well as his, Dominic knew that she was almost there. He slipped his finger inside, stabbing her with two swords. "Fuck me, Fuck me. Oh! Oh! Oh!" Bernadette's hips bucked and she cried his name as she came. Dominic almost came before Bernadette; he moaned her name as she did his.

They held each other, sharing slow kisses implying it was time for a quick break.

As their slow caresses and kisses continued, it was inevitable that it was time to fuck again. They made love until they came the first hint of dawn appeared on the horizon.

"Do we have to leave today?" Bernadette sighed leaning back against Dominic as they lay together, her back to his front.

"Yes, dear," Dominic said. "I'm sorry, my love."

"It's alright," she said, taking his hand from where it was and kissing the back of it. "It had to end sometime. And as hard as it is to leave here, it'll be nice to be back home, in our own bed."

"Yes, ma'am," Dominic said.

They turned on the TV and after a quick embrace. The doorbell rang downstairs shattering the moment.

"Damn…What does anyone want this early?" Bernadette said. "I'll get it," she got from under Dominic's arms.

She opened the door and found Gerard and Amy there.

"Good morning," Gerard said. "Sorry to disturb you so early but may Amy and I speak with you both for a few minutes?"

"Of course, come in. Is there something wrong?" Bernadette stepped aside so they both could enter.

"No, no. Nothing like that."

Bernadette led them into the upper parlor when Dominic appeared at the bottom of the staircase, tying the belt of his robe.

"Darling, Gerard, and Amy have

something they want to speak to us about," she said.

"Oh, isn't it a holiday to talk business?" he said.

"Well, Dominic. It's—"

"Let me tell him," Gerard began nervously while looking at Amy.

"Dominic, Madam Bernadette…. Anthony and I, well—we got engaged last night…" she said, holding out her left hand to show her diamond ring. "We'd like your blessing."

"Ooh," Bernadette said. "Congratulations, of course, you have it," she said as she embraced Amy. Dominic was grinning as he stepped forward to slap Anthony on the back.

"I told you to do this years ago. Didn't I?"

"Yes, you did." Gerard agreed.

"There's no champagne leftover but we have some brandy," Dominic said going over to the bar. He took the bottle and took out four glasses. Once they each had a glass, Dominic lifted his high to toast.

"To Gerard and Amy, may your lives together be filled with more loving than fighting, more laughter than tears and may you enjoy a long and happy life together."

"Cheers, cheers."

"Thank you," Amy said.

* * *

"WELL, we don't want to keep you any longer… I know we all have a lot to do before the cars are ready to leave. We just wanted to share our great news."

"Did you tell Anthony yet?" Bernadette said.

"Yeah, while I was telling him, he was playing his video games."

"That boy—"

"Well, I'm glad you did this. It's been a long time," Bernadette said embracing Amy again. "Congratulations, I'm so happy for you."

"Thank you," Amy said. "It means so much to me to have your blessing."

"Oh, you are very welcome, my dear," Bernadette said. "I hope you know that I look upon you as more than just my partner. You're family."

"Thank you," she said again, moving back to Gerard.

Once Anthony and Amy left, Bernadette turned to her husband. "As much as I would love to climb back into bed with you, we should probably get ready, the cars will be here before we know it."

"Okay dear," Dominic said as he leaned in to kiss her forehead. "I'll put in a rain check?"

"Oh, absolutely," Bernadette said as she quickly kissed him then headed upstairs to shower and start packing.

* * *

THE SUV STOPPED on the tarmac in front of their private jet.

"Thank you, Walter," Dominic said quietly so as not to wake Bernadette who was sleeping.

"You're welcome, sir, it's been a pleasure. Is there anything else, sir before I get the door for you?"

"No, we're okay. Thanks," Dominic said waiting for Walter to get out. Walter opened the door and before climbing out; Dominic shifted Bernadette so that she was lying on the seat. He got out and then reached in to pull her up and into his arms. She mumbled and as he pulled her close, Dominic kissed her on the forehead.

"Anything else I can do to help?" Walter said as he closed the car door.

"Please see to the bags, Walter, thank you," Dominic said quietly as he carried Bernadette to the plane. He quickly went up the stairs, responding quietly to the pilot's greeting as he reached the top. Dominic carried Bernadette past the main seating area to a large room at the back of the plane. Pushing the door open with his shoulder, he stepped inside the room and went to the bed. Using his free arm, Dominic tugged back the covers and then laid Bernadette down, smiling when she rolled onto her side.

Dominic slipped off her boots then he removed her coat, skirt, and blouse then leaving her in only her slip. Then, he pulled the covers up over her, tucking them in around her.

"Sweet dreams, my love," he said before slipping out of the room and closing the door behind.

He headed back to the main seating area and found the pilot ready. Amy, Gerard, and Anthony were already buckled in. Dominic buckled himself in, giving a nod to his bodyguard Pierre when he was ready.

"Ladies and Gentlemen, thanks for boarding. The weather is clear across the Atlantic. We don't anticipate any problems so our flight time home should be around ten hours." The pilot came out to make a last check before heading to the cockpit.

Once the plane was airborne, Amy and Gerard saw Dominic get up to return to his cabin.

"Stay here with us, buddy. She'll be fine," Gerard said.

"I know but I'm feeling a bit tired as

well. See you in a bit"

"Ok. Hey, Gerard, let's head to our quarters. You owe me something, don't you?" Amy said.

Anthony put his hand over his mouth.

"Hey, you stay here and play your little video games, young man. Daddy and Mommy have something to talk about," Amy said.

"Yes, mom."

"Hey, before I go. There's a bottle of old champagne in the galley. It's yours. Go have some. You deserve it," Dominic said smiling.

"Thanks, Bud."

* * *

THE SHADES WERE DRAWN and Dominic stripped down to his boxers, leaving his clothes draped over an armchair in the corner. He climbed into bed with

Bernadette and curled onto her backside. He then pushed back her hair to lean in and say, "I love you" before closing his eyes and joining her dreams.